HOLE IN THE WALL

HOLE IN THE WALL

PAN DEMIRAKOS

Book cover design by Damonza.

For my son and wife; without them I am deaf, blind, and mute.

"To be content with little is difficult; to be content with much, impossible."

— Marie Von Ebner-Eschenbach,

Aphorisms

HOLE IN THE WALL

1

THERE IS a hole in the wall, it's been there since Cecil Gedeon bought the house two years ago, and all he did, instead of fixing it, was cover it up with a painting: a Vincent Van Gogh print of the skull of a skeleton with a burning cigarette. The hole is the size of a dollar coin and located in the basement office of his two-bedroom house, on the wall that separates the boiler, and even though he could use the room for work, since there were plenty of hedge-fund investments and demanding clients that could be managed on the weekend, which would improve productivity and alleviate the hefty workload, he preferred to use his office for pleasure, particularly for watching porn, listening to heavy metal music, drinking lots of alcohol, smoking weed, snorting cocaine, popping prescription pills, and surfing the internet for any depraved curiosities his mind could conjure; much like the hole in the wall, he covered the void in his heart with an image that resembled the Van Gogh.

Cecil didn't come from money, and his education wasn't exceptional, but he was lucky enough to land a job, which through a series of events that included a tremendous amount of lying and massive laziness on behalf of his employer to check up on the facts, where he was making a six-figure salary by advising and administering a series of trust-funds; a job he wasn't particularly fond of, nor was he any good at, but there was no oversight, and as long as people kept making money, he received more and more lucrative quarterly bonuses, which he spent on lavish house parties—and before long, the only part of his life that mattered was those Saturday night get-togethers—in fact, he lived for those parties.

He didn't have any friends or family that were close, but he had plenty of acquaintances, from social media followers to clients, coworkers, drinking buddies, random strangers, neighbors, and they always knew somebody that wanted to have a good time; therefore, there was always a packed crowd of fresh faces to keep his interest growing, all the while the attention he received as the host gave him an air of gravitas. And he provided as much as he could, since his bank account kept burgeoning each week with more coin and he had no respect for savings, although he loathed the fact that others considered him wealthy; any compliment made him indignant and flustered, and he expressed that feeling with a cynical smile, while anybody miserable, he gravitated towards with a quiet grace that made him appear benevolent and charitable, which only contributed to his reputation as a magnanimous man, a grand lie he loved perpetuating.

2

HEXAGRAM, the first track from the self-titled Deftones album, pumps through the airwaves and vibrates from his eardrums into his nasal cavity, where it meets a thick shooting stream of cocaine. Cecil nods to the raunchy rhythm and chases the melody with a shot of whiskey, then lights a cigarette, jumps to his feet, strums his air guitar, and proceeds upstairs to play host for his depraved party; this has been his routine for the past few months, as his tolerance for chopped powder and alcohol has reached a new threshold. He greets guest after guest with enthusiasm and puts his amateur bartending skills into good use, making everybody feel at home. Once the crowd reaches a comfortable size, he socializes with a handful of regulars while making quick runs to the basement in order to partake in substance abuse. Occasionally, he receives a blowjob from a promiscuous girl, his neighbor, Catherine Duvall, a miserable sort of creature that's addicted to sleeping around, whom he doesn't find attractive, except for when he's high or horny, and usually, after such a pernicious act, he has a nasty habit of ignoring her for the rest of the night. Around four in the morning the party grinds to a halt, as Cecil has drunk enough booze to intoxicate a whale; then he spends the next day hungover, trying to puzzle together the pieces, while paranoia rewrites his memories with a colorful temperament, often imagining things that never quite happened.

Sunday was his least favorite day, everything was a mess from the night before, and he was depressed due to the drugs, with his only solace being that late in the afternoon, a cleaning lady came for a few hours to put some order into his soiled chaos; he had forgotten her name multiple times and referred to her simply as Sweetheart, even though there was nothing sweet about her appearance, except for a well-mannered attitude, one might argue (she was always pleasant), and the fact that she couldn't speak much of English made him feel at ease, as there was no need for small talk. Cecil got into a routine of drinking two glasses of Vodka during the methodical disinfecting to clear his hangover and also to get into a pleasant mood while he watched her clean, and in his demented fantasy, he imagined that she must've enjoyed being watched, a wicked thought that felt empowering, and with enough time, he found her ability to clean his house provocative, forming a voyeuristic fetish of a sort.

Monday through Friday was a total blur, since he worked morning until night under the influence of prescription pills and then drank himself to sleep. Not to be entirely drowsy about it, he had brief moments where he wanted to escape from this routine and search for a peaceful existence, which always made him laugh, because it made him think of how boring Heaven must be and that all the fun was had in Hell—and that's where he wanted to go.

3

THE PARTIES BECAME ALL the more popular, and Cecil hired an assistant to restock the supplies, provide all the party favors, and keep a tally of the guests, partly because of paranoia, but it also offered exclusivity to the event that only enhanced the soirée; Sparkplug, a nickname given to him by Cecil during a massive cocaine binge when they first met, was quickly adopted by all the guests, due to his talkative mode when high; the kid was in his early twenties, from the neighborhood, unemployed, living in his mother's basement, and even though he wasn't paid in cash, the parties alone were more than enough compensation. He looked forward every week to mark everybody's name in the guestbook, socialize with beautiful girls, and get blasted with opiates. Sparkplug even adopted the nickname outside of his social circle and embraced the new persona with pride, dropping all of his previous friends with an arrogance that was ill-advised, as his mother cautioned him that real friends were hard to come by. But after a couple of weeks, Cecil became complacent with his assistant, giving him more and more responsibilities, most of them were meaningless and demeaning, like cleaning his shoe collection, or reorganizing all the bottles at the bar in alphabetical order, but some chores were fun, like deciding how much cocaine each guest should snort while waiting in line, a line that stretched from the basement all the way upstairs, and Sparkplug was a vociferous advocate, as he made sure that there was always enough of it in his system to permanently hardwire his brain. Cecil's favorite activity during the snortfest was to sit on the couch with one hand on a whisky bottle and the other tied in Catherine's hair (whose head was resting on his bulge), as he watched each guest load up and pay him respect with a cliche compliment, before returning to the party; he felt like a mythical character, whose loyalty was bought and paid for by the sin provided.

As fate would have it, everything forever changed one festive night when the Van Gogh painting fell to the floor, probably because of the tremendous bass shaking the walls or the foot traffic directly above, and revealed to his guests the crooked hole in the wall; all eyes gravitated towards the imperfection and their reaction was one of innocuous surprise, while Cecil felt an irrational burning shame, as if people got a glimpse of who he really was, a monster, instead of a good man, and then he pushed Catherine's head aside and rushed to the painting, picked it up and returned it on the wall, but the damage to his reputation was done, or so he felt... then, to make things worse, Sparkplug made a crass comment, that he can fix the hole by stuffing it with cocaine, which made everybody in the room laugh, except for Cecil, who took the jest as an offense, and then he walked over, slapped his assistant across the face with a backhand and dragged him upstairs by the ear and kicked him out of the house, and for the first time, stopped the party early. That night, he brewed his anger on the couch while drinking his pain away, replaying the event in his head with an affinity for hate: hate for his assistant, hate for his guests, hate for himself, hate for life, and hate for all that is sacred!

But, alas, a familiar sound awoke him that same night, and it was the Van Gogh painting that once again fell to the floor; he dragged his intoxicated body off the couch, grabbed the painting, and before covering the hole, he took a look inside, and for a brief moment, saw a dark red fiery eye flash and disappear... the shock from the apparition made him perspire a cold layer of sweat... he then rushed to the boiler room, turned the lights on, and examined the hole from the reverse side. Unable to fall asleep again, he glanced over at the hole multiple times throughout the night, while the fiery red eye burned an imprint in his confused mind, forever robbing him of his sanity.

4

Using a putty knife, Cecil fills the hole in the wall with spackle, waits for it to dry, then paints over the flat surface with a red marker, as a stark reminder—even though he covered it in the first place to forget—perhaps it was a strange anomaly that served as a dire warning, that there are things in this world that do not need to be understood and are better left a mystery.

The rest of the week was spent restlessly, as he barely slept an hour each night, while the prescription pills made his heart pound like a drum, giving him the impression that a heart attack was imminent—and he welcomed it—because he felt that to simply suffer in existence was a much worse punishment than death.

To compensate for his erratic behavior from the last party, as an apology, he bought Sparkplug a gift: a used pickup truck that helped him run errands, and then the relationship was amended almost instantly. Soon after, everybody in the guestbook received another invitation, that this week's party will be a special event: Cecil's birthday celebration, regardless of the fact that it wasn't even the right month, and he celebrated the festive lie with the utmost joy, hiring more staff: an actual bartender, a professional dancer, and two servers, which made Sparkplug feel like he got a managerial promotion. This time, the extravagant party lasted until sunrise, and once all the guests left, Cecil respectfully asked Sparkplug and Catherine to stay behind and entertain him for a few more hours, by fornicating, this way he can watch the spectacle while opening his mountain of meaningless presents. He awoke hours later, in the afternoon, by the repeated banging of the front door, which felt like a gorilla was pummeling his gut. Sweetheart started cleaning the house immediately, but this time, instead of watching her scrub and mop, he began helping her without getting in the way, and at first, she found his behavior odd, but she appreciated the movement of furniture, the lifting of carpets, and the collection of trash, and then before long, she acknowledged him as an assistant of a sort, giving him some orders through sign language that made a huge difference, and she was extremely happy to have finished early and that her generous tip far exceeded her entire paycheck.

That week, Cecil used a few of his sick days, since he never took off from work and would lose them anyway at the end of the year, and stayed at a hotel across the street from the local hospital; an improvisational move he didn't expect making until he heard a random conversation while waiting to cross the street about some poor obese fool not surviving a heart attack. It was as if his body was taken over by a malevolent spirit, and all he did was just go along for the ride. He spent most of the time watching ambulances through the second floor window, driving in and out of the hospital parking lot, as he received multiple warnings from the staff that smoking wasn't allowed in the room. When he finally returned to work on Thursday, he was in a much better mood, and all he could think about was the upcoming party and how he could top last week's birthday bash—and then when the ludicrous idea hit him, he began laughing wholeheartedly, in wild spurts, between clients and errands, and he didn't stop laughing until he fell asleep on the following night.

5

THE LINE of people stretched from the front door, through the lawn, out on the sidewalk, and spilled in the street, by far the most crowded party up until that point. Sparkplug was inconveniently stressed by the volume of guests, chain-smoking cigarette after cigarette, while trying to keep count of the incoming traffic.

Then the music suddenly stops, and Cecil climbs on the counter to get everybody's attention; he makes a speech about love, pretty much any cliche he could conjure vomited out of his mouth, then pointed at Catherine, as if a spotlight landed on her, and when he dropped to his knee and revealed an engagement ring, she cried out of shock and joy, screaming yes yes yes at his unexpected wedding proposal. Sparkplug was stupefied by the theatrical act, as he bottled his ambivalent jealousy in the back of his throat with a taciturn smile, while everybody that was waiting on line walked past him, clapping and cheering, and crowded the house like a jar of sardines. Catherine became the happiest girl in the world, and for the next few hours, Cecil treated her with all the respect she deserved. Chairs were broken that night, puke and alcohol covered the floor, and drunk fights were taken outside to reach their bloody conclusion; it was degeneracy at its finest.

A scratching sound fiddled in complete darkness as if a nail was digging through a wall, and at first, Cecil was too wasted to wake up, but a sense of paranoia overwhelmed him; the sound stopped the moment he opened his eyes, and he laid there on the couch motionless for a good half hour. Sprawled on the floor beside, with her face on his foot, was his fiancé, and the fact that she wasn't snoring made him think that she was probably awake as well; he lightly kicked her, and all she did was turn around and mumble. He then turned on the light-switch, and to his dismay, beneath the Van Gogh painting, a streak of thick dust stretched downward to a pile of dust accumulated on the floor. Cecil wiped his tense face with his hands and repeatedly rubbed his eyes to make sure his imagination wasn't playing any games... it took him a few seconds to connect the dots, and he eventually walked over, got on his knees and dipped his fingers in the pile of dust; then he got up, lifted the painting off the wall, and stared at the newly formed hole, which had a slightly wider diameter than before. He was disturbed to say the least, as he rushed to the boiler room to confirm his suspicion that nobody was there. Catherine awoke soon after by an incessant finger poking, and was confused at first with his aggressive stance, as Cecil interrogated her to see if she had anything to do with the perturbing mystery, and she outright denied any involvement, but he didn't believe her, and as a result, an argument escalated quickly where he kicked her in the face for lying, and it would've gotten a lot worse had she not ran to the bathroom and locked herself in. When Sweetheart arrived in the morning, Catherine found the courage to sneak out of the house with a handful of bruised tears.

6

CECIL TOOK the entire week off from work and sat in a chair facing the hole in the wall, expecting to see something; he wasn't sure if it was a monster, a spirit, or his own insanity that was hiding behind the veil. Sparkplug brought over supplies, but was surprised to find out that there would be no party this week, then Cecil gave him enough money to buy Catherine a bouquet of flowers and take her out on a fancy date, on his behalf, to compensate for stomping on her face.

The days went by in a blur, and when Saturday came around, anger surfaced through his intoxicated chakra, and he began trashing the entire house in a wasted fit, only to wake up in the middle of the night in a puddle of puke. Then to balance his mood, he drank more vodka, crawled back in the chair, and began speaking to the hole in the wall with a delirious apprehensive tone, mumbling about random events that took place during his childhood, mentioning his abusive father and how he deserved to die in that car accident and how his mother should've been in the seat beside, as a series of pent up memories from adolescence carbonized in his mental furnace; and then he began to laugh, more than ever, as he realized how insane he sounded, while urinating right there in the chair, which was a warm decompressing relief.

Until all of a sudden, bolts of electricity shoot through his veins, as he noticed that the edges of the hole were slightly vibrating... and he focused his attention at the anomaly... and the hole appeared to be breathing at the same pace as his lungs. He then got up close and felt the warm breath hit his face. The smell elevated his testosterone, as he salivated like a wild dog, then he touched the cracked surface, and it was not hard or concrete anymore, instead, it was soft and squishy, as if it were alive. He had done enough acid and mushrooms in his life to know when a hallucination was taking place, and reasoned that this must be an effect triggered by the horrific chronic substance abuse, then he did something unexpected, and like an animal, he stuck his index and middle finger in the hole and felt the moist warmth. The organic pocket began reacting to his sensitive clockwise rubbing, and before long, his finger was covered in a thick clear jell. Enamored by the perverse activity, he curiously tasted the excrement, and there was something erotic in the flavor, to the degree that it gave him a mild erection, and in his deranged madness, he ripped his clothes off and started fondling himself, as the hole made a loud industrial moaning sound. He then dragged the couch beneath the gap, climbed on its tight upholstered back, and feverishly shoved his hard phallus inside the manifested womb, thrusting himself against the wall and achieving an explosive orgasm in a matter of seconds; afterwards, it was the first peaceful night of sleep that he had all year.

7

"MONDAY? How could it be Monday? Where did Sunday go...?" Cecil kept asking himself, as he dragged his naked body into the shower and laid in the tub to recuperate his stamina, unable to fathom that he slept for thirty-six hours straight, he knew that he had to hurry and go to work, but he lacked the energy and motivation, even though he recognized the urgency in the voice of his coworker on the phone, as clients complained, some even asked to be reassigned to a more responsible manager or else they would leave for a greener pasture.

He popped pill after pill, and that was sufficient enough for him to trudge wearily through the day. Half of his clientele had already abandoned ship, but fortunately all of his top whales were still loyal to him, at least for the time being. Still, he could not focus, his frail mind was consumed by the mystery of the missing day; it was impossible for him to comprehend that he slept for that much. During his lunch break, he called Sparkplug, and was informed that any attempt to answer the phone or door the day before was met with absolute silence, and then Cecil promised to give him a copy of his keys, in case something like this ever happens again. He wondered if there might be an underlying medical condition that prompted the deep sleep, but he ignored that thought since he didn't care too much about his health. When he returned home, the cataclysmic mess was overbearing, and in his desperation, he called Sweetheart and begged her to come over for a late-night cleanup, as he repeatedly apologized for not answering the door the day before and even offered to pay her three times as much, and with that detail, she reluctantly agreed.

He took a quick shower, shaved his face and body, popped his pimples, and wore an expensive suit. While she cleaned, he interrupted her with a delicate nudge and politely asked for them to have dinner after she finishes—as a thank you—and she categorically declined, mentioning with not so many words that her husband wouldn't approve of that type of behavior, but he passionately insisted in his own charming way, with a sense of urgency and desperation, allowing for her to finish early enough to keep him company for a short period, and with much hesitation and reluctance, she eventually agreed to the impromptu dinner. He ordered an assortment of meat, appetizers, and two bottles of wine from his favorite steak house, and when the food arrived, he set up the elaborate meal on the table and lit a bunch of candles to enhance the atmosphere. She semi-blushed with his jubilant effort, and although she knew the whole thing was rather inappropriate, after a couple of glasses of wine, a pleasant smile shaped her lips. There wasn't much talk, but they communicated more than they ever had by merely staring in each other's eyes, which was akin to the observation of the ocean under a full moon. He wanted to love her, badly, like a feral animal, to ravage her with his mouth, but he knew that that would only spoil his long-term objective, and to simply seduce her with small gestures was a far better strategy. Before departing, he gave her a warm minute-long hug, and she eased into his arms, accepting the inappropriate nature of the transaction with a smitten longing for affection. Afterwards, his heart was palpitating in a wash of adrenaline, and then he drowned the butterflies in his stomach with a layer of tequila, as he fantasized about the unbecoming affair all the way until its tragic conclusion, which was to steal her away from her husband and then dump her on the side of the road, a terrible act that was extremely rewarding.

For a few hours, he had forgotten all about the hole in the wall, but once his cruel fantasy lost steam, the disturbing memory of his encounter with the mysterious entity returned with a vengeance; he was then filled with a denigrating apprehension; it bothered him immensely that he partook in such a deviant sexual act with something so vulgar, and that he derived pleasure in shoving his cock in the wall, that plaster and paint turned him on, and then he rushed to the basement in a flurry to check up on the shape-shifting hole, to see if a feeling like that would ever resurface again, but this time, the texture of the cavity appeared normal and brittle, instead of slimy and organic, and the only feeling that arose was that of disgust. He was then lost in a vacuum, between what is and what if, and he hyperventilated until a cold layer of sweat covered his brow, which was followed by a terrible rash with no relief no matter how much he scratched. He briefly considered speaking to a therapist, or to check-in at a psych ward, but he was afraid to face the grim realization that he might be mentally ill—and then he suddenly blamed the half-empty bottle of tequila in his hand—that perhaps he's been drinking too much, and that maybe he needs to take a break.

The self-loathing ran its course near the bottom of the bottle, then he stumbled into the boiler room to examine the hole for the umpteenth time, to ease his paralyzing neurosis, as his mind raced across a multitude of wild theories, eventually giving up on the paranoia altogether due to catatonic exhaustion. His only obvious solution was to fill the hole up again with even more spackle—but then—as he grabbed the putty knife, he was shocked by a revelation; he noticed a small three-foot metal door behind the boiler that wasn't there before, and that's when his absurd sense of humor returned with might and main, and he laughed until his insides were aching from the pulsating stress, forgetting all about his desire to cover the hole.

8

It took him two whole days to open the new door, as he savored the Delphic mystery, even briefly considering the possibility that the door might've always been there, hiding behind the boiler, and that he was too stupefied by his consumption to ever pay any attention, but deep down inside he knew he was only fooling himself, and he allowed his imagination to stretch across the infinite potential of his wicked mind: his final guess before opening the door was that it probably didn't lead anywhere and that the entire thing was some kind of a cosmic joke, perhaps perpetrated by himself during a wasted fit, a Mephistophelian prank executed to perfection.

When Cecil turned the knob and the door creaked open, a spine-tingling wave ebbed from his fingers down to his toes, and what he saw was a staircase that led straight into darkness; he took a moment to soak in the fear, and then rushed back to his office, grabbed a flashlight, and returned with an exuberance fit for exploration, as he walked downstairs and discovered a giant room twice the size of his basement office. The walls were bare brick, newly placed, with no outlets or electrical wiring in sight. He was perturbed... how could this room be down here without his knowledge? He then called his realtor and asked about a second basement, that he might've possibly overlooked when the contract was signed, but she denied any such thing and even found his question strange and concerning.

He finished the workweek without losing any more clients, but was hesitant to throw another party; instead, he invited a construction crew to paint the walls of the new basement, install electrical wiring, and move in a few pieces of furniture: like a pair of couches, a minibar with stools, and a king-size bed. The following week was spent in this strange crypt, fantasizing about its potential use and how he could take advantage of the extra space.

Who would've thought that the hole in the wall would have such a positive influence on his psyche? And he welcomed the idea that the offspring of his sexual endeavor with the house was this new room, a wild concept that was beyond reason and rationale, as the portentous abstract thought that the Devil was as powerful as God was guiding his lack of faith in the wrong direction. When he felt ready to introduce his discovery to the world, he invited Catherine and Sparkplug over for dinner, and even though he could sense that there was a newly formed personal connection between the two, he was confident that he still commanded their unyielding loyalty and that they would do anything he asked of them. After a few bottles of aged cabernet, he giddily explained that there is a hidden room in the house that they absolutely must see, and when he led the way through the small metal door and downstairs, they couldn't believe their eyes and were shocked that they weren't privy to this area beforehand. Cecil apologized for not being honest (by not being honest), and then got on his knees and bluntly begged them to move into this room and become roommates—and with no hesitation, they both said yes! The rest of what happened are just details: Catherine spent the night pleasuring her fiancé with her mouth, while Sparkplug obediently entered her waste export tunnel from behind.

9

THE NEW BASEMENT proved to be a huge hit for the party, providing enough exclusivity and mystery that people could not stop talking about its sudden appearance, as more guests crowded beneath ground than above, even the boiler room was packed with misfits, and the drugs flowed from body to body like nectar in a beehive. That unforgiven night ended in an unplanned orgy, as the guests unclothed and banged all over the place, while Cecil couldn't fathom the conclusion, except to credit the dark pornographic event to the spirit of the house, whose occult force must've influenced the depravity in each of the participants. When Sweetheart arrived in the morning and witnessed the smut, she made a u-turn and left the house in horror. Cecil chased after her and vomited excuse after excuse, that he wasn't part of the act and didn't know about it until he arrived just a short while ago, but she couldn't see past his lying, and declined any financial offer he made to return at another time. Because of this tragedy, he kicked all the naked bodies out with a broomstick and then ordered Sparkplug and Catherine to clean his house in her stead, which wasn't exactly the same, but it was better than nothing.

A profound soul-wrenching depression consumed him at work, and all he wished for was worldwide annihilation of all that is living. Fire and brimstone was in his eyes, and he pulled his hair until chunks of it were left in his hands. He hated the fact that he lost his cleaning lady, even though his house was cleaned by somebody else, and couldn't believe how stupid he was to allow for such a sexual act to take place, while the paranoia that his benevolent reputation might be ruined pushed him an inch closer to the edge. Burning hot revenge ran through his veins and he wanted a reason to act on it, as he walked around town after work for hours each night in search of mayhem, destroying window displays and scratching cars with a screwdriver any chance he had, only to wind his expanding emotion into a gordian knot.

Cecil ordered Catherine and Sparkplug to remain in the basement after midnight and went as far as even making a threat that he would murder them if they dared disobey. He then sat in his office chair and brewed his suppressed anger over a bottle of Vodka, privately, squeezing his jaw with enough strength that he tasted the blood seeping from his gums; when he felt comfortable enough to disassociate himself from his maddening obsession, he removed the Van Gogh painting from the wall and stared into the hole; he didn't have to say anything, as the darkness liberated his mind and excited his anxious loin. He got up close, shut his eyes, and waited a considerable time until the familiar industrial breath blew on his face, and then the outflow of erotic smell sent goosebumps across the expanding stretch of his skin; when he eventually opened his eyes, the hole had transformed into the shape of a feminine mouth... and he was in pure awe... as he felt the strange lips with his tongue, which gave him a powerful arousal. He then dragged the couch underneath the mouth, and in a rush, climbed atop, unzipped his pants, and plugged his erect manhood straight into the proverbial wall-socket—and that's where he took out his frustration—as he slammed against the concrete with such might, that he bled from the tip, and he couldn't stop pouncing until achieving a glorious climax, regardless of the excruciating pain, as he made so much noise, that his roommates beneath almost came up to check on him, had it not been for the strong mental hold he had on them; instead, they wondered what hellish demon had possessed his flesh on this night and whether he'd still be himself come tomorrow.

10

CATHERINE WASHED the blood on his groin with a wet shirt, as Sparkplug slightly shook him and whispered in his ear to wake up. When Cecil came to his senses, he ordered the pair to return to the basement, without an explanation, but unable to understand the reason for their sudden dismissal, they protested and refused to obey, which triggered him, and then he threatened to poke their eyes out with a screwdriver if they don't do as their told, which scared them to submission. In his naked paranoia, he searched the house from room to room for any surprises, hoping to find some kind of a new door that would lead to another area, but after searching everywhere, moving all the furniture away from the walls, and circling the outside perimeter twice, he was frustrated by the terrible disappointment. While a few neighbors witnessed his nakedness, which made him feel exposed and vulnerable—and when he ran inside to throw a robe on, a terrifying thought zapped the column of his spine, that perhaps the discovery he was expecting to find might be in the basement beneath! And then he darted downstairs, tripping on the way, as his heart was two beats ahead of him. Catherine and Sparkplug saw how deranged he was and stayed out of his path, even though they volunteered to help him find whatever he was searching for, but he didn't pay any mind and instead barked at them to go upstairs and let him be—and they happily obeyed, out of fear that he might lash out or hurt them.

Cecil flipped the bed over, ripped the sheets, stomped on the couch, punched a hole through the minibar, smashed the stools on the counter, and then started screaming at the top of his lungs, viscerally, like a wild animal stuck in a hunter's trap, as he dug his fingernails deep in his forehead, painfully penetrating the surface of his skin, in a deranged attempt to rip his face off; but once he saw streaks of blood in his hands, a calming sensation washed over his temperament. From the corner of his eye, he noticed the only spot in the room that was overlooked, and he quickly dropped to his knees, grabbed ahold of the carpet and flung it in the air, finally discovering what he was looking for: a trapdoor that led somewhere (perhaps to a third basement!), and he was bursting with utter joy, as he howled upwards in a delirious bipolar expression, rubbing his hands until they were red hot, and then he delicately lifted the newly minted metal door from the latch... and what he saw on the other side was another sharp rustic staircase. This time it was made of a charcoal-colored stone, and led deep beneath the foundation. Then, with a flashlight in hand, he embarked on a journey to the nether-realm, as the staircase kept descending without a room or an exit in sight! He counted each step at first, more so out of a tepid nervousness, but lost count once he crossed over a thousand... he then suddenly stopped, and in an effervescent state of deliriousness, looked back at the tiny light at the surface, as the cold sweat dripping from his face and lack of oxygen gave him the impression that he was about to pass out at any moment—and he soon realized that if he didn't abandon the expedition and return at a more opportune time with a portable oxygen tank, he would die.

When Cecil finally returned to the surface, he was physically and emotionally drained, and covered in a dark soot mixed with blood, mold, and sweat. As he laid on the floor to recuperate his mind and body, nothing made sense anymore, except that he must be stuck in some kind of a nightmare somewhere between purgatory and Hell. About an hour later, he crawled upstairs and discovered that Sparkplug and Catherine had left, which was a pleasant relief, as he wanted to keep the secret affair and metamorphosis of his precious home to himself. Then, after a cold shower, he bitterly remembered that he was late for work.

11

CECIL PACKED his backpack with a pack of cigarettes, a zippo lighter, a sandwich, a chocolate bar, some chewing gum, a bottle of water, a quart of whiskey, an eight-ball of cocaine, two joints, a small container of pills, wired earplugs connected to a music player, a roll of toilet paper, a Swiss army pocket knife, a flashlight, and a portable oxygen tank; and off he was to the races, determined to reach the bottom of the never-ending staircase. This time he reached fifteen thousand steps before calling it quits, as he realized that he needed an even bigger oxygen tank, perhaps a pillow to rest, and a long enough rope tied to the top that would help him ascend, since the climb back almost crippled him. He was absolutely certain that there must be a bottom at some point, stubbornly applying rationale when there was clear evidence that none applied. After his second failed expedition, a flu-like respiratory illness put a temporary brake on his obsession, incapacitating him for nearly two weeks, and out of sheer frustration, he gave up on his maniacal pursuit, vowing to never reach the bottom, stubbornly, as if he was punishing the house by not abiding to the curiosity that was calling out to him.

He had received multiple warnings from his boss that his job was in jeopardy and that if he didn't get his act together soon, he would be fired, and in response, he made every promise under the sun and even signed a document acknowledging the end of the line and that at the next hiccup they would amicably part ways. The house parties temporarily stopped, and he made an honest effort to recuperate some of his sanity: the drinking was met with a strict limit of two glasses of wine per night, the coke was put on hold, relying only on weed to curb the edge, and the pills were counted and timed to a strict regiment. His condition improved almost immediately, and glimpses of innocence surfaced on his skin in the form of pimples, or so he thought.

But like in all tales of absurd despondency, loneliness eventually crept in through his orifices, and he developed an irrational itch that he couldn't quite scratch, as he kept calling Sweetheart every other night to come over and clean his house, until she blocked his number altogether, and that nearly broke him, as he wept and yearned to numb the pain by returning to the former days of excess, regardless of the consequences. He flipped open the pocket knife and sliced small inverted crosses on his forearm, as the sight of blood was a worthy distraction, which led to a break of all the rules, and just like that, he was instantly sucked back down the drain of consumption, as the relapse devastated his fragile psyche and he unraveled into a delirious state of paranoia. He had fought hard to convince himself that the hole in the wall was a product of his imagination and that the additional rooms were merely a fabrication, but not anymore, once he was wasted, a sense of clarity returned, if one can call that clarity, and he realized that the reason he felt irrational was because he ignored that which he knew to be true, that he had developed a relationship with something, something that lived inside the house, and it was about time for him to reacquaint himself with that fulfilling notion of destiny, a sick and twisted sentimentality. He grabbed ahold of the Van Gogh painting and ripped it to shreds, then bunched up the pieces of paper and hungrily shoved them down his throat in a cannibalistic effort to eliminate the enemy! Free of his self, of all the warnings he had placed, it was just him and the hole now.

12

CECIL TALKED to the hole in the wall on a nightly basis, developing his esoteric connection with the spirit into a strange bond of burden, confessing all of his secrets, desires, dreams, regrets, and aspirations, he even poured alcohol and cocaine down its vacuous crevice —and every time, the intimate interaction transformed into a perverse rub and tug, as the troublesome foreplay incorporated any phallic object that could be used as a sexual prop, from a toothbrush, a screwdriver, to bananas, cucumbers, carrots, metal rods, and branches; and on many nights, surprisingly, he was even left rejected. It was as if on certain occasions the house was playing hard to get, painfully teasing him to the edge but leaving him hung and dry, and that drove him even madder, as he obsessed to the point of losing sleep entirely.

Weeks passed without him leaving his basement; all the food delivery drivers had to enter the unlocked house and meet him by the staircase. His skin turned sickly pale, and a nasty rash covered his body, with gashes all over from the relentless scratching; it was a honeymoon period straight from bondage, while an alarming infection on his most prized possession prevented him from using his tool for the foreseeable future; he knew he had to go to the doctor immediately, but he dreaded leaving the house. Eventually, one fine morning, the pain was insurmountable, and he was forced to crawl out of his cave and enter a cab. As he was leaving the neighborhood, he turned around with an agoraphobic longing, looked at his house, and was pleasantly surprised to discover that it had grown two whole floors, with a pointy roof atop that made it the tallest structure in the neighborhood; an overwhelming pride flushed through his veins, temporarily eliminating the burning pain in his groin. He had avoided exploring the house up until that point, stubbornly, but now he couldn't wait to return from the doctor's office to explore his creation. Multiple prescriptions for antibiotics and painkillers were given by the doctor, and some sound advice to stop any activity that caused the infection in the first place, which was ignored.

He marveled at his accomplishment from the front lawn until sunset, while all the neighbors looked at him with an ominous curiosity from behind the safety of their fences. They couldn't understand how the house was built so fast without them paying any attention to the construction crews, and then, within days, a reputation developed that the man inside must be up to no good, and that perhaps, someday, he could be a danger to the entire neighborhood—even though the temporary cessation of the parties was a blessing for all who had grown irritated by the weekly late-night activities. Cecil could sense the prying eyes, but he didn't care.

The house had transformed into an eight-bedroom mansion, with three bathrooms, two kitchens, two living rooms, two balconies, a backyard with a shed, an attic, and a massive dining room, and although there was no furniture in place, except for appliances, which he found somewhat endearing, he appreciated the fact that the house left the decorating up to him—and the preferred style of choice was vacancy, as he loved vast empty space. That night he celebrated by drinking, eating, snorting, jumping, kicking, punching, running, and dancing in every room as if he was a lifelong patient in a loony bin. All that was left now was for him to throw another party.

13

CECIL APOLOGIZED for treating Sparkplug so indignantly and then invited him to the party, not as an employee, but as a guest—and that if he didn't show up—he would understand. And then the boss did all the organizing himself, invited every guest, bought all the supplies, in a manner that proved that he could do the job better than his assistant, which was a ludicrous notion, sparing no expense, hiring bartenders, dancers, servers, and choosing a theme, that of a secret society, requiring all guests to arrive at the masquerade in proper attire: a robe and a mask. He even planned a surprise: a mock human sacrifice executed by a cohort of strippers pretending to be high-priestesses and a virgin, and went as far as to hire an artist to create sculptures of owls that belong to the

Canaanite God, Moloch. Giddy madness was his only expression, as he proudly bragged to the hole in the wall that he would be king one day and that this house would become his castle. Then, due to his many insecurities, he went ahead and placed a sign on the basement door that read: All trespassers will be shot, no exceptions—bang bang!

He greeted every guest with a firm handshake, while people kept asking him about the sudden development of the house: how he built it so fast and secretive. And he gave all the credit to his contractor, whom he chose not to disclose. When Sparkplug arrived with Catherine at his side, holding hands, Cecil became jubilant, rushed forward, and kissed both on the cheek, then he publicly begged for forgiveness, as he explained that the time apart had cured him of his miserable paranoia (he was specifically happy to see his fiancé still with the ring on her finger), and he promised that when the time is right, he would speak frankly about all of his terrible secrets, that he will come clean to regain their trust and respect again, and that everything will eventually make sense. They pleasantly nodded along, looking forward to bridge the gap of discontent. Then, once midnight came around, the ritual began on the top floor, and everybody squeezed in to catch a glimpse of the show, as the strippers exhibit quite a pretentious portrayal, with cheesy memorized dialogue, a ton of perverse props, buckets of fake sugary blood, and a violinist who dramatized the event with classical notes.

The only person absent from the event was Sparkplug, and that unnerved Cecil, even though Catherine was there, mesmerized by the pornographic show. He had to find his old assistant and bring him upstairs to share this experience, to record his reaction, and after searching every room in the house, his pulse palpitated faster at the thought that he might've disobeyed his clear order and went to the basement—which sent chills down his spine—and finding the door unlocked, he knew that that was the case. His entire demeanor changed into a crooked, shriveled expression, as a dark cloud settled above his eyebrows. He took his time descending the stairs, like a slithery predator, and when he saw Sparkplug standing an inch away from the hole in the wall, enamored by the indubitable force of darkness, he licked his lips and slowly snuck beside him, and wasn't acknowledged until he spoke —at which point, Sparkplug jumped back and mumbled that the hole in the wall was whispering into his third eye, warning him that he should leave this house and never return—but he could not believe any of it, and thought that he had lost his mind. Cecil confirmed his terrible suspicion by admitting his own experience, how he and the hole have a special relationship, and that the sudden expansion of the house into a mansion was the fruit of that endeavor.

Sparkplug was stupefied, cold sweat formed on his brow, as his mind had a hard time processing the information. Cecil comforted him with a pat on the back and then led him downstairs to share a bottle of whiskey, to calm the nerves, while he answered any crazy questions he might have. The story encompassed the events so far, and when the discovery of the trapdoor with the never-ending staircase was mentioned, that was the furthest Sparkplug's feeble mind was willing to entertain, as he began to push-back on the narrative and was more inclined to believe that they were both crazy, then admitted that he'd heard enough and begged him to stop pulling his leg —an insulting notion that resulted into an argument —then Cecil offered to show him the controversial staircase as evidence, and Sparkplug agreed to see it, reluctantly. He pointed to the trapdoor beneath the carpet and ordered him to open it, and when Sparkplug did exactly that, Cecil casually took a step forward and shoved him with all his might down the stairs, and watched him roll into the endless abyss, while the sound of bones breaking echoed all the way back to the surface. He closes the trapdoor and covers it again with the carpet, then returns upstairs to catch the ending of the ritual. Afterwards, he stands at the front lawn and thanks everybody for coming to the party, keeping Catherine at his side, as she temporarily pretends to fill the role of his loyal fiancé.

14

CATHERINE LEFT NO STONE UNTURNED: she first went to Sparkplug's house, questioned his mother, tracked down all of his old friends, and after three days, she even informed the police; she was heartbroken, while Cecil comforted her with alcohol and drugs, repeatedly blowing smoke up her skirt, that Sparkplug was jealous of him and ran away, which made little sense, for many reasons, but after enough repetition, she eventually believed her fiancé and surprisingly felt resentful, going as far as calling her friend a weakling and a coward for leaving without ever saying goodbye.

Two weeks passed, and their relationship imitated that of a married couple: spending nights on the couch watching movies, ordering food, and not leaving each other's sight. Cecil gave up on his job altogether, figuring that he was probably already fired, and believed that the house would provide whatever he needed whenever he needed it—for his ego was bigger than himself, bigger than the planet, he was part-God. Catherine respected his request to stay away from the basement, and every night, he took advantage of the excuse that he had to work in his office and not be bothered; his man-cave was precious to him, that's what he kept repeating; but dismally, for the time being, the hole in the wall did not tease or arouse him, nor did it put up with his flirting or fondling. At first, he enjoyed the coy game, figuring that the house might be jealous of his fiancé, a charming sentiment—and yet, he was curious to see how long this game would last—so, they temporarily enacted boundaries and pursued the path of friendship: a man and his hole, a twisted sitcom if there ever was one. There were also times where he yelled and screamed at the top of his lungs, but the bipolar outburst was short-lived, and Catherine never questioned his behavior; she knew that some things were better left unsaid.

He did try telling her the truth once, in a desperate plea for help, while they were wasted and high, but she didn't pick up on the cues, and instead turned his outcries into cruel jokes, that he was a house-fucker and a twisted puppy in need for a walk, which reminded her of a friend she had in high school that fucked the exhaust pipe of his car until he got so sick that they had to cut his weaner off, and then she admitted that in her youth even she had shoved plenty of strange objects up her vagina that had no business there, regretfully so, prompting him to give up on the notion of being saved altogether—he was so far from redemption that it appeared as a distant star. As a last resort, a confrontation between his fiancé and his mistress was arranged, and he brought Catherine downstairs to have sex in front of the hole in the wall, to see if he could get some kind of a reaction, but he was sorely disappointed, which ruined his mood, and then he couldn't bring himself to climax, as he blamed the booze and the coke for the impotency. The next day, he bought another replica of the Van Gogh painting to cover the hole, and even went as far as to spackle the gap again—only to recreate it on the following night with a screwdriver, making it twice as big. All of his efforts capitulated into a prolonged weeping, as he cried and begged for the hole to love him again, and that he was really really really sorry for playing childish games.

In his descending madness, he had great aspiration for his castle to grow so large that he would reach the clouds and border the kingdom of Heaven, only to invade and destroy the Creator with a poisonous kiss on the lips! Catherine couldn't understand the source of his immeasurable sadness, and to compensate, she figured that an elaborate surprise party behind his back would cheer him up—so, she used the black book to the best of her ability and told everyone that it was a potluck, hoping that a massive feast might be precisely what the doctor prescribed, food for the soul.

15

When the first guest arrived holding a tray of lasagna and a six-pack of beer, Cecil was dumbstruck by the generosity, and yet he was furious that Catherine would throw a party behind his back—and all he wanted to do was to punish her for the insubordination—but he remained quiet and played along, since even more people walked toward his front lawn; the commotion was jarring, and he was busy shaking hands until every surface in the kitchen was stacked with plates of food. Then, at some point, to relieve his pressure-cooked frustration, he did the unthinkable, he grabbed a paper plate of mashed potato and threw it across the room, hitting his fiancé straight in the face, and surprisingly, instead of shock, the crowd exploded with laughter, which encouraged her to grab a plate of chicken wings and return the favor, and with that slight adjustment, a massive food fight ensued—and that's when the party really took off like a bottle-rocket on the fourth of July—it became a war zone, resulting in a truly comestible mess of smashed chow and irresistible aromas, only to run out of edible ammunition soon after, and as a result, they ordered even more food from a catering hall and every delivery place in the neighborhood. It was the most fun that he's had in a long time, and he thanked his fiancé with a sloppy drunk kiss for the wonderful surprise.

But, but but but, in the morning, an unexpected visitor knocked on the door, and that's when the third and final act of Cecil Gideon's fable began, when a city employee arrived to take a long hard look at his building permits. Cecil was unwilling to cooperate at first and tried to chase the woman away with unflattering epithets, but after a few warnings: that the situation could escalate to the eventual confiscation of his property, he reluctantly agreed to let her inspect the premises, and she was immediately grossed out by the dried food on the walls and slippery floors. The note-taking was abundant, and her many questions received no clear answers, except an I don't know or an I don't have it, which frustrated her immensely, as she nodded along all over the house and even below, ignoring the hole in the wall—but insisting for the trapdoor to open—and that's where he drew the line, repeating over and over again that the key was lost, that it's simply a storage closet a couple of feet deep. Unless he broke the latch or called for a locksmith, which he wasn't willing to do, there wasn't a chance in hell that it would be opened. She stopped bickering, since she had seen more than enough, and all the violations had extended to a second page. In the end, she was frank with her conclusion, admitting that he would receive a series of fines and a court date, and was implicit that he should comply and get a lawyer, if he has any hope to resolve this mess and keep the property—and all he could do was nod along with an antagonizing smile, as he wondered which of his neighbors did him dirty.

For the next few days, he rang the bell to each house in the neighborhood with zest and fervor, to pettily explain his situation in order to get some kind of a reaction—and he narrowed the rat down to two suspects—while Catherine did her best to convince him not to retaliate because that could land him into even bigger trouble, then he suddenly turned the tables on her when she least expected it and painted her into an enemy, blaming her for everything under the sun, and even went as far as to accuse her of ratting him out to the city, as revenge, for what he did to Sparkplug, which shook her to the bones. And she was lucky enough to escape his house in one piece, as he chased her around the living room with a belt buckle. If it wasn't for a chopping knife in the kitchen drawer she grabbed at the last second, she would've suffered immensely—and that was the last time he ever saw her.

16

THE HOLE in the wall kept him comfort in the darkest of times, and Cecil was glad to have exchanged a physical connection with a paranormal one, as there wasn't room for both. The house finally responded to his pent-up needs. He vowed to never again bring a third party into the relationship, promising exclusivity from now on like a devout husband who had momentarily strayed off path, and then the house spread its tight fertile tenderness for a wild night of sweaty bareback wall-pumping. He became a dutiful servant, continuing the expansion of his temple at a fervent pace. Within a week, the house had grown into a four-story twelve-room mansion with a pool in the back. But the drugs were running out and the alcohol was down to a bottle of rum. He hadn't eaten for days and his skin had turned to an almost translucent pasty white leather with black circles around his bloodshot eyes; one would think that he was on the verge of death, if not for his obsession, which kept his spirit aflame and made him determined to bear his cross to the top of the mountain.

The neighborhood was spooked by the sudden development of the mansion. A local television network stopped by for a report, some locals were interviewed, and although Cecil refused to make any comments, the final piece was so successful that it was syndicated nationwide, and the acknowledgment gave him immense pleasure. That alone was a cause for him to throw another party, to show off his masterpiece, but his funds were depleted—and that was impossibly frustrating—then he temporarily considered asking for his job back, possibly accept a demotion, but he knew that that would be pointless... then he briefly considered renting some rooms, but the money wouldn't be enough either... also, he was concerned that the house might object, and the last thing he wanted was to jeopardize any further expansion. Daily, he had begged for his lover to create money out of thin air, and every morning he searched every drawer and closet, but it only enhanced his desperation. And then, one day, a letter was dropped in the mailbox, in it was a bill from the building department for all the unpaid fines, the amount was upward of two hundred thousand dollars, much more than he ever anticipated, and then he suddenly became blind with rage, as the prospect of losing his mansion collapsed his lungs and made him incapable of breathing for a good minute and a half. He desperately yearned to burn the entire neighborhood, to massacre every single one of his neighbors.

The court date was in two months, and so, out of hopeless despair, he called everyone, explained the situation, and personally invited each guest to the party: a fundraiser that would allow for more parties in the future, by providing an exclusive membership to all those who donate. Most of the people showed up, but with the drugs and alcohol depleted, they left early, and he only managed to raise a few hundred dollars. It was the first party that was a dud, and that was a massive blow for his ego. He needed money fast, and he had no way of earning it, or a place he could borrow it from. He hated the mansion for dragging him into a trap, but, at the same time, he couldn't live without the fruit of his effort, his only purpose in life was to serve his home, to maintain and love it, and then, he unexpectedly bit his forearm out of sheer frustration and ripped off a chunk of skin, which numbed his entire body and cooled his temperament. For a brief moment, he managed to think, and the only thought in his rotten head was to rob a bank, a far-reaching idea that must've been inspired by a movie, probably one with a bad ending.

17

CECIL SPENT days researching the heist; he visited most of the banks in the state, narrowing down the favorable ones that yielded the best potential for success, took notes on the security guards, cameras, transactions, escape routes, and fumed with discontent at the many unfavorable scenarios. He considered searching for partners, but didn't know anybody trustworthy enough. The internet was the only source for information, by analyzing previous successful efforts, he was planning to mimic others that had gotten away with the loot, but he lacked all the resources to repeat anything ambitious. On the surface, he read that many bank robbers were caught right away, but also the clearance rate was a whopping sixty percent, and that gave him a glimmer of hope, as he considered himself smarter than average. Ideally, he would prefer to dig a hole underground and break in at night, but that was just fantasy. His effort would need to happen in broad daylight, the old-fashioned way, with a handgun purchased from the black market with the last of his cash; he knew the whole thing was risky and most likely a huge mistake, but he was plagued with despondency, and that maybe even secretly, he didn't care if he was caught, he just wanted for this whole drama to end one way or another. Preferably, he would rather witness a nuclear bomb explosion up close and disappear into the ether, only to reincarnate as a cockroach.

Wearing a wig, an old striped suit, aviator sunglasses, and a fake glued mustache that hung crookedly on his upper lip, he walked into the bank with a gun in his jacket pocket and a paper note that read: "This is a robbery. You have one minute to empty the vault and bag all the money, or else I'm gonna kill everybody here, starting with the security guard and then with you!" But as he got in line, one quick look at the security guard made his stomach churn, and then he ran back out to the parking lot and vomited between two cars. He wiped the cold sweat from his brow, removed the mustache, gulped a bunch of massive breaths, while a sobering shock made him reconsider everything. He didn't even know if the money would be enough, except that it might buy him some time to find the rest—if only somebody were there to stop him—as he stared at the truck, which he planned on using for his escape, he briefly missed his old friend, then he remembered what he did to him.

There were a handful of people in the bank, and he measured every single one while waiting in line for the teller. When his time came, he walked to the counter and delivered the note. The teller read it, turned pale, discreetly emptied the cash from the register into a bag and then went inside to collect the rest from the vault, while the manager was busy with a client, and at that moment, Cecil felt fortunate that his simple-minded plan was going to work. The teller returned in a hurry and slid the hefty bag over the counter. Cecil took it and casually walked outside, while nobody paid any attention, then he ran to his car and drove away like a bandit. He could not believe how easy it was, as he glimpsed in the bag and saw stacks of hundred-dollar bills, euphoria had filled his heart, while he nervously looked at the rearview mirror for flashing lights. There was nobody following him, just him and the road, but then, suddenly, a ticking sound coming from beneath the cash alerted him, and a pink-colored gas fumed through the opening of the zipper and filled the car with a bitter-sweet chemical smoke. He rolled open the windows in order to breathe, as pink trails stretched in the wind. He then dumped the truck on the side of the road, near the woods, wiping as many prints as he could with disposable alcohol wipes, and then walked to the nearest bus stop about two miles away and waited for the bus, covered in a pink hue.

18

FEVERISHLY SCRUBBING his face in the shower, Cecil removed the pink paint, in addition to a thin layer of his skin, then he delicately washed each hundred-dollar bill, and separated the clean ones from the damaged lot, as he spread the wet paper across the floor. The amount was thirty-one thousand dollars, just a fraction of what he really needed, but he figured, if it was that easy to get, all he had to do was repeat the crime enough times until he reached the desired amount. But alas, a police siren can be heard approaching in the distance, and a numbing sensation smacks him in the gut, as his mind reverses course, and he questions everything... he could clearly see how foolish he was and how this ridiculous pipe dream of reaching Heaven's door has utterly ruined him. He should've sold the mansion to pay the debt and escape from a life of constant debauchery straight into a peaceful existence; it would've been a second chance, to transform from a wolf back into a sheep. All the while, deep down inside, underneath all the mental dirt, he yearned to serve a higher purpose, to serve that which he knew to be true, instead of the monster of his own creation. He understood that no real satisfaction derived from the mansion, except for the expansion of his ego, it was all pyrite: fool's gold, which masked a deluded sense of freedom, a grandiose self-will that was narcissistic to the core, but now it was all over, the dream had transformed into a nightmare, as it usually does. He had crossed over the rubicon and was cursed not only for life, but also in the afterlife, and that made him laugh to the point of tears.

The police sirens never reached his front porch, and that peaked his interest; he then rushed to the window, peeped through the curtains, and what he saw was five police cars parked in front of Sparkplug's old house. Cecil watched the cops raid the place from both entrances and drag the old lady out in handcuffs, as if she was her son's accomplice in the robbery, and at first, he was ecstatic to have avoided calamity, but a thought crept in his head, that before long, he would be next, it's just a matter of time before he gets caught. So, he collected the money in a rush and considered escaping to the airport... but he couldn't... he couldn't come to terms with abandoning his significant other; like a victim unable to leave his kidnapper, an irrevocable jealousy consumed him, that somebody else would take over his beloved asset, and his conscience couldn't allow for such an egregious act, while a drawn out animalistic weeping swelled his eyes with a slimy slurry of tears. He was trapped between madness and delusion, he could not pay the debt, at least not in its entirety, and even if that bought him extra time, he was terrified to rob more banks or commit other crimes... the untenable walls of reality were quickly creeping in on him, and at that moment, he was struck by a severe panic attack and the world around him went dark.

When Cecil gathered his senses, he crawled to the window, and the cops weren't there anymore, and that loosened his lungs enough for him to breathe better. Feeling like he had been sober for too long and that a typical drug overdose would solve all of his problems, he punched a hole in the wall, then crushed and snorted a piece of plaster, drank a bottle of rubbing alcohol—and that's when he had his final inspiration, one last grand hurrah: a party that would end all parties, themed after his favorite fictional event, titled: Ragnarok—which was the cataclysmic destruction of the cosmos and everything in it, even the Gods.

19

Cecil begged everyone on the list to make it to the party, as he highlighted the importance of the event by making promises on drugs, liquor, dancers, and entertainment; while he spent all of his stolen money, except for the pink-stained denominations, on top-shelf product, and due to the sentimental value of all the previous parties, this event was more packed than ever before. He made sure to have at least one brief conversation with each guest, shake their hand, and thank them for coming. Once the celebration was in full swing, he retired into his office to spend the night with his hole.

After some jibber jabber, his elevated mood gravitated down the drain, and he blamed the hole for setting him up for failure, for stroking his ego, for sucking his blood, as he steadily increased the consumption of Jack and cocaine until he stopped speaking altogether, while he hovered between the two planes: of consciousness and subconsciousness—and that's when the hole responded—first in the usual manner, tempting and teasing him for one last sexual endeavor, to amend the animosity and convert his hatred into a perverse love-making act. But he rejected the offer, and instead asked for a divorce, so to speak, a separation of man and material, and in that moment, he realized that he would rather go to jail for life than to submit to a demon. He vowed to come clean and confess everything to the authorities first thing in the morning—and he would humbly serve his time. Then, the tectonic weight slid off his shoulders in an emotional earthquake, as he begged God for forgiveness, praying for the first time in his life to find his will to live, to endure the pain, to be a decent man again, and not a degenerate nihilist, to break the habit once and for all, and he feverishly smashed the empty bottle of whiskey on the wall, badly cutting his hand, then grabbed the bag with the pink debt notes, wobbled over to the hole, and shoved the stained cash straight into the vaginal darkness! The hole grew with each insertion until the bag was empty, and then he screamed inside the head-size cavity, that that would be the last of his offering! But the hole had other plans; a shadow-shaped face that mirrored his own crept out of the darkness and jolted him—and his aggressive stance was instantly infused with unfathomable fear—then the shadow jumped out of the hole and replaced his own silhouette, becoming a part of his movement, as he kept fighting with something that wasn't materially there. Adrenaline overpowered the high and he ran upstairs, pushing everybody aside, and made it out to the front porch, where he realized that he couldn't escape from his own shadow no matter how hard he tried... and then understood that there was only one thing he could do, and that was to destroy the enemy once and for all! And so, he ran back inside and screamed at everyone to leave, that the party was over, but nobody took his plea seriously, until he lit up the window drapes with a lighter, and then the fire and smoke created a massive stampede.

Cecil watched the fire spread to the ceiling, while he heard voices of demons screaming through the foundation of the mansion; the joy of wiping the slate clean unshackled him from bondage. When the fire became overwhelming, he ran to the exit, grabbed ahold of the sizzling knob—but it would not turn—then he grabbed a chair and threw it at the window, and shockingly, the window did not break, and he repeated the effort with even more strength and yielded the same result. The mansion had trapped him in the oven. Some people attempted to break in to save him, but the fire was impregnable. He knew he had minutes to live and that his breaths were numbered; the only area that was not clearly burning was a path that led to the basement, and with each step forward, fire covered his freshly pressed footprints, as he rushed downstairs. There was only one place he could go, straight into the belly of the whale, and he opened the hatch and walked down the never-ending staircase; he walked for as long as he could keep his breath, then lost his balance and stumbled forward, and when he used his hands to get a grip, he took another deep breath and realized that he could still breathe, which was a temporary relief, but what confused him was the white light from the fire above that illuminated brighter and brighter by the second, as it covered all the walls and went past him and downward into the abyss, all the way as far as his eyes could see, it was a beautiful sight. While peering down the narrow corridor, he saw a silhouette slowly moving upward... he cautiously approached the figure, and the contour was that of a man, soon enough he realized that it was his good friend, Spark-plug! And for a brief moment, he was really glad to see him, as he jolted downstairs for a quick embrace, until he got up close and had a better view of his eyes, and in them was the void of a soul, the emptiness of God, the nothingness that exists before and after the spark, and the animated lifeless corpse scared him more than death, as it symbolized the sin of man, the ultimate truth, stemming from the disobedience in the consumption of the forbidden fruit from the tree of knowledge of good and evil, and instead of surrendering to his punishment, as he had yearned for, he feverishly rushed back up toward the light and jumped headfirst into the fire, straight into the arms of the creator.

ACKNOWLEDGMENTS

Special thanks to my friend Shaun Vaughn Timm for telling me about his Taxi Driver moment, where he stood in front of the bathroom mirror and had a deranged conversation with himself, which served as the inspiration for this story.

ABOUT THE AUTHOR

Pan Demirakos is a jack-of-all-trades, and although his first love was always writing surreal fictional stories, he is confident and proficient enough as a performer, director, and producer. Equipped with an occupational studies associate's degree from The New York Conservatory for the Dramatic Arts, his deep understanding of character development, especially when paired with his profound imagination, make him an exciting voice in the indie community. As a filmmaker, he has worked on many Hollywood productions, short films, and music videos, where he wore every hat under the sun, from production assistant to executive producer; in addition to his voracious appetite of writing screenplays, he has written many poems, songs, and commercials, while his personal artistic highlight happens to be a concept album composed in his youth, a Rock and Roll opera akin to American Idiot, regarding the discourse of our modern age. In his free time, Pan loves traveling the world, making music, reading the classics, talking to random people, and learning from all the masters that have a nugget of wisdom to share.

Please leave a review if you have a minute, it helps with getting the book out to a wider audience, thanks!

SCAN ME

amazon.com/~/e/B08ZVNB6CD
instagram.com/habbit
facebook.com/PDemirakos
twitter.com/PDemirakos
linkedin.com/in/pdemirakos
youtube.com/peterhabbit
pinterest.com/peterhabbit
bookbub.com/authors/pan-demirakos

COMING SOON

Smitty Gets Away with Murder!
A Novella

Smitty Lamortea comes from a long line of serial killers and all he wants in life is to find a nice girl to brainwash into becoming his significant other, so he can finally appease his tyrannical mother and continue the murderous trend for another generation, just like nature intended; this family satire is a cautious parable that poses humanity's beastly desire to kill and eat meat against the infinite moral landscape of creation by dissecting the meaning of the forbidden fruit into a vegetarian nightmare.

SMITTY GETS AWAY WITH MURDER!

CHAPTER ONE

A saw ripping through meat dances to the tune of Happy Birthday playing from a laptop; the aftermath of a party gone horribly wrong is filled with cheap decor, blood splatter on the wall, spilled drinks on the floor, and a stack of presents underneath the portrait of Smitty Lamortea on the mantlepiece. The bedroom door opens and the merrymaker himself steps out, naked and drenched in blood, pumped by the workout of dismemberment, which adds dimension to his natural athletic physique, all the while he's exhilarated from the adrenaline of eliminating all of his guests with a stainless steel butcher saw. He enters the bathroom, leaving behind a trail of bloody footprints, and takes a shower. When most of the gunk has flushed down the drain, he steps out and grabs a towel from the hallway closet; on the second shelf is an embalmed human head, he looks at the fixed eyes with affection before taking a seat to open his presents.

The post-party celebration continues into the night; Smitty drops a paper bag on the island counter, consisting of french fries and a cheeseburger. The bun is flipped over and a splash of poison splatters the meat.

In public, Smitty is incognito, displaying a decrepit persona marred by a limp leg and a semi-paralyzed face; he walks in the darkness like a wolf in sheep's skin, parading the paper bag, in search for a victim that might be hungry enough to accept food from a stranger.

Underneath an overpass littered with piles of garbage and debris, a persistent knocking rattles a homeless man that was asleep in a cardboard box; he crawls out like a dirty snail, mumbling to himself about the hole in his shoe and the constant water seepage.

Crouched half-way, with a pseudo-pathetic disposition, Smitty says: "Sorry for waking you up, buddy, but I bought a cheeseburger deluxe from the diner across the street without knowing that my poor wife had already baked beans for me at home—how dumb am I?"

"You need to get your head straight, mister. You can't be wasting money like that, especially when you got a woman at home cooking for ya, or else she's gonna find some other poor fella to feed," and he cackles, crookedly, "but I appreciate taking me into consideration, all kidding aside, you're a good man, thanks a bunch, I'm starving like a fiend," and he grabs the food and greedily devours it.

With the cold intensity of a white shark circling an injured seal off the coast of the pacific, Smitty mentions: "My father always said that hunger was made by God in order to feed the Devil; he wasn't an intelligent man, but he sure was poetic. He said that hunger shapes us all, from the way we look, feel, and even think, that it determines our purpose. We all depend on hunger, and no matter how many times we feed the inner beast, hunger will return for more, until there's nothing left except a shadow of something that used to walk and take a shit."

"Tell me about it; I'm hungry all the time, like I got

a leaky gut or something," and he shoves the last of the fries in his mouth.

"More importantly," and Smitty stresses the point by raising his index finger, "hunger teaches us that killing is okay—in fact, it teaches us that killing is necessary."

"Ain't that the ugly truth? Hunger is the root of all evil," says the homeless man, reaffirming the absurdity, as he wipes his mouth with his shit-stained sleeve and licks his lips, but then, all of a sudden, violent convulsions take over and he bangs on his chest for his lungs to pump more air, turning blue in the face, and dies from asphyxiation, in a slow, agonizing expression.

Aware of the incoming perambulatory resurgence of the sun in the wee hours of the morning, Smitty figures that one last stint might put the cherry atop on an otherwise festive celebration, and to regurgitate an old fetish of his, a medical cooler that was recently stolen from an HIV research facility at the expense of a security guard who tried to prevent the theft, lands on the kitchen counter; dry-ice seeps from all sides as it opens, revealing a bag of contaminated blood; the toxic red plasma pours into a plastic bucket, followed by a box of sharp metal thump-tacks, and then a wooden spoon spins the mixture.

Wearing construction gloves, Smitty glues the bloodied spikes on the bench in angles where people might sit on, and when the train makes a full stop at the next station, six hipsters enter and take a seat; each one gets pricked in a musical order, putting a smile on his demented face.

In a sketchy neighborhood, where nobody should wait for public transportation, Dora Coolidge rests her head against the pole of a bus stop after an exhausting night of turning tables. She lifts her heels ever so slightly above her shoes to ease the constant throbbing and thinks about the first thing she'll do when she gets home, which is to take a hot bath and drink a glass of dry red wine while watching the birds chirp through her small bathroom window, an experience more rewarding than the money she earned, but as fate would have it, that bittersweet longing for relief from now on will only exist in memorial, as a chloroform rag wraps around her face from behind, and without much ado, she passes out into a conveniently placed wheelchair, and Smitty wheels her away.

He parks the fresh catch in the corner of the shaky elevator and they ride up to the fourth floor. When he finishes duct-taping her legs, arms, and mouth, he carries her from the couch into the bathroom, where she wakes up in a panic, forcing him to drop her head-first into the tub.

Outside the local flower shop, Smitty looks at the plants on display, and his eyes gravitate toward a small cactus; the owner allows him to take it free of charge, having heard rumors of a neighborhood demon lurking around for attention, out of boredom. Smitty places the plant on the shelf above the toilet, in an angle that receives minimal light, and then holds his gaze on Dora's panicked face.

As the moon rotates into the throne of the night sky, Smitty prepares steak tartar for his new acquisition, until the ringing of the doorbell interrupts his culinary mode, and asks: "Who is it?"

Officer Chan replies: "It's the police; we're looking for Smitty Lamortea."

He walks from the kitchen into the living room, wiping his hands with a rag, and asks: "How can I be of help?"

Officer Warren answers: "We'd like to ask you a

few questions, if you don't mind, can you please open the door?"

"Sure, yeah... uno momento por favor..." and he quickly sets up a small ladder in front of the storage closet, rigged with a mechanism that plugs into a socket with a button underneath the third step that electrocutes anybody standing on it, tests the current and feels the vibration run through the ladder, then places a bottle of air-freshener and an empty plastic water bottle on the counter, and finally turns on the humidifier, pressing a code on the interface that illuminates the transition of a small red light into green. He composes his malevolent self in the mirror, opens the door, and charmingly says: "Sorry for the wait, officers! You caught me in the middle of cleaning my oven—please, come in!"

After a quick interior scan of the living room, officer Chan asks: "You live here by yourself?"

"I do—still enjoying my life as a bachelor—it's hard finding a good girl these days."

"You don't look like the type that has a hard time getting lucky," says officer Warren, trying to bate him into admitting more than he should.

"Luck is a matter of belief, and unfortunately, I lack the faith."

"I'll keep that in mind next time I go to the casino," making his partner chuckle.

"Speaking of Casino, maybe you know my brother? Short guy, big mouth, lots of charisma. He's an avid casino goer himself; you can find him in Atlantic City practically every weekend."

"And who's your brother?"

"Oh, he's an officer of the law like yourselves, one of the good guys," but withholds his tongue from further jest, to avoid increasing the already raised suspicion, and explains: "his name is Leon Lamortea, and he works downtown, at the fourteen, everybody loves him, even though he ain't too bright and a bit of a coward when it comes to shooting his gun, but he always takes care of his friends, very loyal guy."

Officer Chan removes a pad and pen from his back-pocket and suspiciously asks: "And how exactly does he take care of his friends?"

"Money, favors, you know, everybody has preferences these days."

"Good to know," and he records that detail on the page.

"So, what brought you, fellas, all the way into my apartment?"

Officer Warren meticulously answers: "A man

matching your description was seen pushing a woman in a wheelchair into the building last night."

"That's..." and he blows hot air out of his thin lips, "terrible... just terrible."

"Why is that terrible?"

"I could only imagine, cops don't come knocking unless something bad happened, right?"

Officer Chan asks: "Are you saying that something bad happened to that woman?"

"That's not what I said."

"What are you trying to say?"

"Nothing in particular, just guessing—did you guys check the cameras in the hallway?"

Officer Warren replies: "We did, they're disconnected."

"My gosh, I've been in danger all this time, and I had no idea, that's just... unacceptable," portraying fear in his eyes, "thank you for letting me know; I'll be more careful from now on."

The cops look at each other, a bit perplexed, and then officer Chan asks: "Before we leave, mind if we take a look at the rest of your apartment? Just so we can say that we did our job."

"Of course, mi casa su casa," replies Smitty, but then, suddenly, he sniffs and pretends to smell something putrid, "oh, man, do you smell that? I'm so sorry... Goddamn baked beans!"

"I don't smell anything."

"Me, neither," says officer Warren.

Smitty grabs the air-freshener and spays it in front of their faces and they jump back in disgust, due to the sudden inhalation of something that did, in fact, smell putrid.

"What the fuck was that?" asks officer Chan, waving his hand to clear the mist.

"I'm so embarrassed, I don't think the beans were baked properly—my sincerest apologies—I should've left them in the oven for at least another hour."

The smell, which was akin to rotten eggs tinged with battery discharge, has disorienting effects, and officer Warren complains while coughing: "Damn... my chest is burning..."

"Crap... everything is spinning..." and officer Chan rubs his eyes, "I can't see straight..."

Smitty raises his shoulders, displaying a complacent smirk in a totally clueless fashion, and nods.

Officer Warren notices something strange: "Hey... are you holding your breath?"

Smitty shakes his head, dramatically, then grabs the empty water bottle from the table, opens it in his mouth with his teeth and discreetly sucks the air out.

"Motherfucker is holding his breath! Shit! Fuck!" And he unholsters his gun and aims it at the suspect, who calmly raises his hands above his head and kneels, while officer Chan stumbles to the bedroom, clears it, and then rushes to the bathroom, where the shocking sight of the girl in the tub is the last image he sees before fainting into oblivion.

Made in the USA
Las Vegas, NV
10 May 2023